ge in the ark

Madeline Valentine

Alfred A. Knopf ⌐ New York

For wonderful Turner

THIS IS A BORZOI BOOK PUBLISHED BY ALFRED A. KNOPF

Copyright © 2014 by Madeline Valentine
MR. POTATO HEAD® & © 2013 Hasbro, Inc. Used with permission.

All rights reserved. Published in the United States by Alfred A. Knopf, an imprint of Random House
Children's Books, a division of Random House LLC, a Penguin Random House Company, New York.
Knopf, Borzoi Books, and the colophon are registered trademarks of Random House LLC.

Visit us on the Web! randomhouse.com/kids
Educators and librarians, for a variety of teaching tools, visit us at RHTeachersLibrarians.com

Library of Congress Cataloging-in-Publication Data
Valentine, Madeline, author, illustrator.
George in the dark / Madeline Valentine. — First edition.
p.   cm.
Summary: A little boy overcomes his fear of the dark during a daring teddy bear rescue.
ISBN 978-0-449-81334-8 (trade) — ISBN 978-0-449-81335-5 (lib. bdg.) — ISBN 978-0-449-81336-2 (ebook)
[1. Fear of the dark—Fiction. 2. Teddy bears—Fiction.] I. Title.
PZ7.V25214Ge 2014
[E]—dc23
2013042362

The illustrations in this book were created using graphite, gouache, and colored pencils on watercolor paper.

MANUFACTURED IN MALAYSIA
November 2014   10 9 8 7 6 5 4 3 2 1   First Edition

George was a brave kid.

In fact, he was braver than most.

But bedtime was a different story.

Every night, it was the same routine.

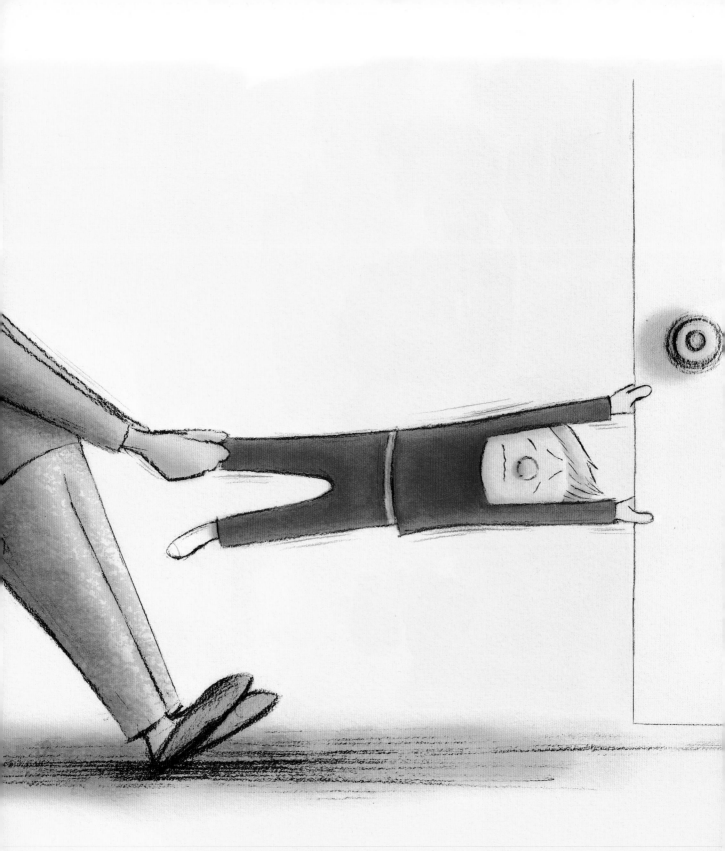

His parents were fed up.

"There is absolutely nothing to be afraid of!" they told him.

"You have your bear to keep you company. And if you wake up your sister, you will be in big trouble, mister."

In the dark, George
did not feel brave.

In fact, he was terrified.

George hid under the covers and reached over to squeeze his bear.

But it was nowhere to be found.

"Oh no!" said George. He looked all around.
Even in some of the scariest places.

Then he saw it. In the scariest
and darkest place.

All alone.

George wanted to scream. He wanted
to call out for his mom and dad.
"Poor Bear!" said George.

He tried to get his bear back the easy way. But it was no use.

He would have to go rescue it.

"I will be brave," said George.

George was daring.

George was courageous.

George was *almost* fearless.

George swooped his bear up from the
darkest place and ran. He held on tight.

"There is nothing to be scared of," he said.

And George felt very brave.

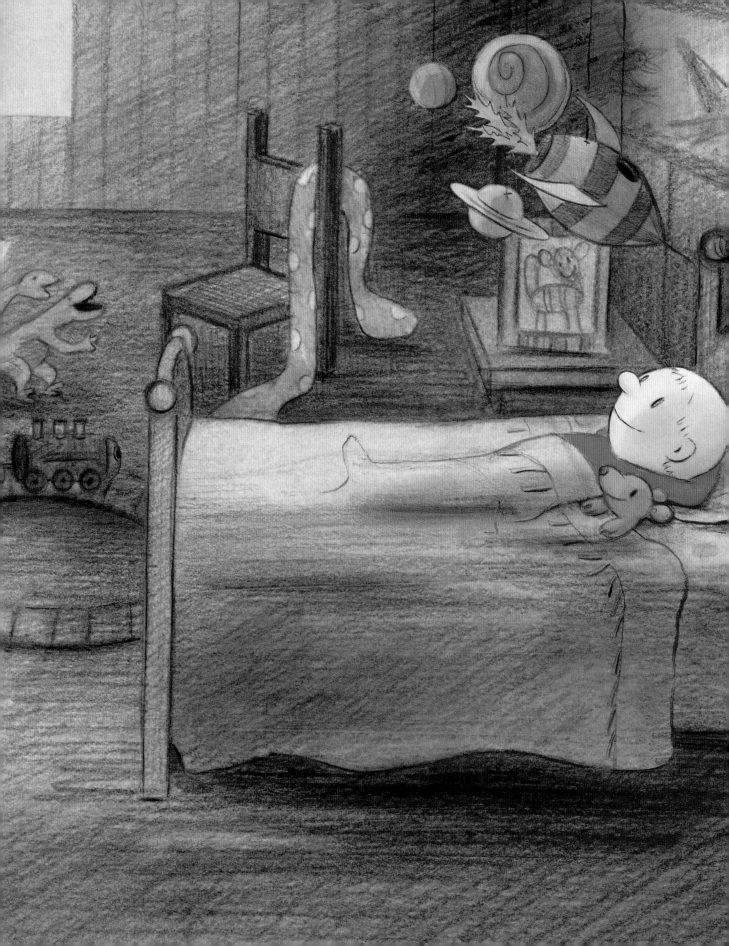